T0063248

AUNT ANNIE'S GHOST

AUNT ANNIE'S GHOST

Ann Westmoreland

authorHOUSE®

AuthorHouse™ LLC
1663 Liberty Drive
Bloomington, IN 47403
www.authorhouse.com
Phone: 1-800-839-8640

© 2014 Ann Westmoreland. All rights reserved.

No part of this book may be reproduced, stored in a retrieval system, or
transmitted by any means without the written permission of the author.

Published by AuthorHouse 08/07/2014

ISBN: 978-1-4969-2950-1 (sc)
ISBN: 978-1-4969-2951-8 (e)

Any people depicted in stock imagery provided by Thinkstock are models,
and such images are being used for illustrative purposes only.
Certain stock imagery © Thinkstock.

This book is printed on acid-free paper.

Because of the dynamic nature of the Internet, any web addresses or
links contained in this book may have changed since publication and
may no longer be valid. The views expressed in this work are solely those
of the author and do not necessarily reflect the views of the publisher,
and the publisher hereby disclaims any responsibility for them.

CHAPTER ONE

"No, THAT'S CRAZY, Aunt Annie," Mr. Jenkins said into the phone. "People don't just up and die at will."

Jenny was listening to her father. It was almost her bedtime, but she hoped to stay downstairs long enough to hear the rest of the conversation.

"I know you said it wasn't your will, but still, the idea's a little crazy. I can't quite understand what you're telling me."

Argo, Jenny's nanny, stopped reading the evening newspaper and looked up at Mr. Jenkins. Jenny wished that Argo would be so interested in the conversation that she'd forget about bedtime until her dad got off the phone. She didn't want to go to bed. She wanted to know what was happening.

"I know, I know," Mr. Jenkins said into the phone. "Your clothes are already on the chair and a note as to how you want your hair fixed is on the table. Yes, yes, I'll take care of everything. Don't worry. Are you sure about this? Well, good-bye. You know that I love you. I'll see you there, but I'll miss you until I do." Mr. Jenkins had tears in the corners of his eyes.

By this time, Mr. Jenkins had captured the attention of Jenny's sister, Marylou. Jenny, Marylou, and Argo stared at Mr. Jenkins when he hung up the phone. They all were interested in the conversation that had just taken place. He turned around and said, "I just had the craziest conversation with Aunt Annie. She said that God had spoken to her, and that she was going to be in Heaven with Him tonight."

"What?" Argo asked, surprised shock in her voice.

"Not only that, but she laid out the dress she wants to wear to her funeral and wrote down instructions as to how she wants her hair combed. She was going to take a bath, wash her hair, and set it in curlers, so she'd be ready."

"That's the craziest thing I've ever heard," Argo commented. "People just don't know when and where they're going to die."

"Aunt Annie thinks she knows," Mr. Jenkins answered. "She believes it."

"Has she called Paul, yet?" Argo asked.

"Yes. She called him before she called me. I'll call him at the hotel and see what he thinks." Mr. Jenkins punched in some numbers on the phone. After a few seconds he asked, "Paul, did Aunt Annie call you?" After a pause he said, "I told her the same thing. Do you think I should go over there?"

Argo put down the newspaper and stood up. "Jenny, Marylou, it's your bedtime."

"Just one more minute, please?" Marylou whined.

Mr. Jenkins hung up the phone. "My brother doesn't think it's anything to worry about. He's been living with our aunt for a long time. He should know."

"Scoot, girls," Argo said in a firm voice.

Jenny and Marylou stood up and walked toward the stairs. Argo had been their nanny long enough for them to know when she meant business.

After Jenny and Marylou were dressed in their pajamas and had brushed their teeth, Mr. Jenkins kissed them goodnight and pulled their covers up to their chins. He told them not to worry about Aunt Annie, that everything, one way or another, would be fine. "My aunt has lived a long time and has been sensible most of that time. I believe that she believes she had a visit from God or one of His messengers." He kissed each girl again and turned out the light.

"Would you please leave the door open a crack?" Jenny asked.

Jenny and Marylou whispered to each other about the strange conversation on the phone, for neither girl understood the meaning of what their dad told them. They were just as confused as their dad and Argo.

The next morning, while Argo combed out Marylou's hair, the phone rang. She put down the brush and answered it on the second ring. "Hello, Paul. How's Aunt Annie?" There was a short pause. "What! She's really dead? How did it happen?"

Jenny stopped eating her cereal and stared at Argo. Argo's face had turned chalk white. She shook as she sat down at the kitchen table and held the phone with a tight grip. Jenny noticed that her knuckles had turned as white as her face.

"Who's on the phone?" Mr. Jenkins asked, coming into the kitchen.

"Uncle Paul," Marylou whispered. "Aunt Annie's dead."

"What?" He took the phone from Argo's extended arm. "Paul, what happened?" Mr. Jenkins' face tightened as he listened to his brother. "An asthma attack? Didn't she use her inhaler?" He paused and listened again. "It was sitting on her nightstand unused? That's crazy!" He listened again.

"A smile on her face? She must not have suffered then." Mr. Jenkins looked relieved. He said good-by after he told Paul that he would come right over. The two brothers needed to make the funeral arrangements together.

He hung up the phone and turned around. "The doctor said he believed Aunt Annie died of an asthma attack, but she didn't try to use the medicine on the nightstand, for the inhaler was new and unopened. When Paul arrived home from work this morning and found her, she was lying in bed, dead, with a big smile on her face."

"Did she really have a visit from God?" Jenny asked, her eyes wide.

"I don't know for sure. But something happened that made her very happy. I guess we'll never know, not in this lifetime anyway." He picked up a cup of coffee, kissed Jenny and Marylou, and walked toward the back door. He turned and smiled. "Bye, girls. I'll see you this afternoon."

Jenny put her cereal bowl and her juice glass into the dishwasher and ran upstairs to get dressed. She couldn't wait to tell Bonnie, her best friend, about Aunt Annie.

CHAPTER TWO

THE SATURDAY AFTER Aunt Annie's funeral, Mr. Jenkins announced at breakfast that he had made arrangements to move.

"Move? Where?" Jenny asked. "I don't want to move. I like it here."

"Uncle Paul wants us to move in with him."

"What about school?" Marylou moaned. "I'd have to change schools. What about my friends?"

"Yes, you would have to change schools," Mr. Jenkins smiled. "But, as far as your old friends, you could call them and have them over to spend the night. Don't worry, you'll make new ones in no time at your new school."

"Why do you want to move there?" Argo asked, looking over her coffee mug.

"Paul and I each inherited half the house from my father when he died. Dad told Aunt Annie that she could live there as long as she wanted, rent free. It's a big house, much bigger than this one, and I wouldn't have to make house payments. We could sell this house and use the money for other things. Anyway, that house has been in our family for many years."

"Would Uncle Paul still live there?" Jenny asked.

"Oh, yes," Mr. Jenkins answered. "We'd move in with him. The house belongs to both of us."

"Would we have to be quiet all day, so he can sleep?" Marylou asked.

"As long as he has his night job. But normal living wouldn't bother him. He's a pretty sound sleeper. Aunt Annie had her piano students there most afternoons, and that didn't seem to wake him."

"Can I have my own bedroom?" Marylou asked.

"Sure," Mr. Jenkins answered. "There're five big bedrooms. Everyone can have their own room."

Marylou smiled. She wanted her own bedroom. It was crowded sharing one with her little sister. Jenny took up so much space with all her toys and collections. Now she could have her space and her things.

"Can Bonnie come and play?" Jenny asked.

"Sure, anytime," he answered. "We're not going to be that far away."

"Well," Marylou pondered, "it probably won't be that bad. When are we moving?"

"Next week." Mr. Jenkins looked at Argo.

"Next week!" Argo's eyes widened. "There's so much to do, so much to pack."

"Don't worry about packing, Argo," Mr. Jenkins reassured her. "I'll have the moving company pack everything."

"What about the furniture that's already over there?" Argo asked. "Your Aunt Annie collected so many antiques, and we have a houseful of furniture. How will we ever manage?"

"I'm going over this afternoon and decide with Paul what we're going to keep. We can blend most of our furniture with several of the antique pieces in the house already, and we can store some things in the attic, until we decide what to do with them."

"I love that attic," Jenny squealed. "There's some really cool stuff up there."

"Antiques, yuk." Marylou scrunched up her nose.

"Don't worry. I won't put any antiques in your room." Mr. Jenkins smiled.

"Good," Marylou said. "I like new stuff."

"Can I have that cool bookshelf with the glass front?" Jenny asked. "I can put my doll collection in it."

"May I have, not 'can I have,'" Argo corrected.

"Okay. May I have that cool bookcase?"

"I don't see why not," Mr. Jenkins answered. "We'll all go over there tomorrow after I get home from work. You girls can pick out your bedrooms, after Argo picks hers." Argo had been with the family so long, that she was Family and was considered in all matters.

Argo looked over her mug and smiled. "Thank you."

"I want you to be happy. You do such a wonderful job with the girls, this is the least I can do. Oh, and don't worry about Paul. He's been a bachelor for a long time. He's used to taking care of himself."

"Oh, I wasn't worried about that. Cooking for five isn't much different than cooking for four. He'll be included in everything we do."

"Thanks, Argo." Mr. Jenkins picked up his coffee mug. "I'm more than sure he'll appreciate that."

"May we take the swing set?" Jenny asked.

"Of course," her dad answered, "and Snoopy, too."

Snoopy, the cat, looked up from his food dish.

Jenny finished her juice, then announced, "I'm going to see if Bonnie can play. I have to tell her about moving."

Moving day arrived. Jenny and Marylou woke up early to the sound of the washing machine. By seven o'clock the house was bustling with excitement. Argo had washed the third load of bedding, so it would be clean to put on the beds in the new house. Mr. Jenkins was in the garage. He put his tools in boxes and threw away unneeded things. Jenny and Marylou ate their breakfast in paper bowls and watched the movers pack up the remainder of their dishes. They had packed most of the Jenkins' belongings the previous day.

"Am I going to school today?" Marylou asked.

"No, dear," Argo smiled, "not unless you want to say good-bye to your friends. I thought I'd enroll you in your new school tomorrow."

"I said good-bye to everyone yesterday and gave them my new phone number. I'd rather watch the movers." Marylou jumped when a mover dropped a pan.

"Be careful," Argo warned the clumsy mover.

"Sorry, ma'am," the man answered.

"Can Bonnie come with us?" Jenny asked.

"Not today," Argo answered. "She can come and play in a few days. I'll give her mom the address."

"Okay." Jenny tipped her bowl and spooned up the last bit of cereal.

The movers finished packing and loaded the furniture into a huge truck. Jenny rode in the big cab, with Argo and the movers, to the new house.

"Are you sure you know the way?" she asked. "Did you pack my toys? Did you take Snoopy's litter box? Did you get my bicycle? Did you..."

"Hang on, young lady," the driver laughed. "I believe we got everything. If you see that we forgot something, we'll go back and get it, okay?"

"Okay." Jenny was silent for the rest of the ride. When the truck stopped in front of the big, yellow house, Jenny tumbled out and ran to the front door, calling, "Uncle Paul, we're here! Are you glad to see us?"

Uncle Paul opened the door and stretched out his arms to Jenny. She jumped up and hugged him. She put her arms around his neck and wrapped her legs around his waist. "I'm so happy you're moving in, Jenny. This house is just too big for one person. Come on in. I just finished vacuuming your bedroom."

"Did you put the shelves with the glass front in my room?"

"No," Uncle Paul answered. "I thought I'd let the movers carry it upstairs."

"Okay, I'll tell them." Jenny wiggled out of her uncle's arms, jumped down, and ran down the sidewalk.

The rest of the day was busy with moving things. The whole family was exhausted and tumbled into bed as soon as it was dark. Jenny snuggled down into her bed in her new room and closed her eyes, thinking how she would arrange her dolls on the new shelves. She wondered if Marylou missed her, for this was the first time they hadn't shared a bedroom since Jenny was born. Jenny missed talking to Marylou, but she enjoyed having her own room, a place that was hers alone.

Chapter Three

THREE WEEKS HAD passed since Jenny and her family had moved into the big yellow house with Uncle Paul. Jenny and Marylou made new friends, their old friends had come to sleep-overs, Argo had adjusted to the new kitchen and met some ladies in the neighborhood, Uncle Paul had adjusted to living with a bigger family, and Mr. Jenkins had painted the porch. Everyone seemed happy and content.

One night, about midnight, things changed.

Jenny awoke with a start. She thought she heard music. Maybe her dad fell asleep and didn't turn off the television in his room. She got up and tiptoed down the hall to her father's room. There were no sounds. Uncle Paul was at work, so it couldn't be him. There were no sounds coming from Marylou's or Argo's rooms. Strange. Jenny rubbed her eyes and walked back to her bedroom. Maybe I dreamed music, she thought. She remembered dreaming about a blue devil chasing her when she was little. Jenny thought that was real, too, even after she woke up. She crawled back into bed, pulled the covers up over her head, and curled up into a little ball. That devil dream still scared her.

The next morning, between mouthfuls of cereal, Jenny asked her family if anyone had heard any music in the middle of the night.

"What kind of music?" Argo asked.

"Music from a piano."

"I didn't," Argo answered.

"Me, neither," Marylou said.

"Maybe you dreamed it," Mr. Jenkins suggested.

"Well, maybe. But it seemed so real. It sounded like the music Aunt Annie used to play in church."

"Sometimes when we miss someone, we tend to dream about them," Argo said. "I dreamed about my brother for a long time after he died."

"I dream about your mother all the time," Mr. Jenkins revealed.

"I do, too," Jenny said, "but this was different."

"Don't worry your pretty little head about it," Argo told her. "The mystery will be solved."

"Okay," Jenny answered. She took another mouthful of cereal, but she couldn't stop thinking about the beautiful music she had heard the night before.

That evening, Mr. Jenkins had a phone call from Mrs. Johnson, who lived next door to the church. She insisted that late last night, she'd heard organ music. "It came from the church sanctuary and sounded just like when your aunt played for our church services. I sure do miss her. Thelma Adams tries, but she can't seem to play the way Annie did." Mrs. Johnson went on to ask if anyone had a key to the church that could play the organ.

"Not that I know of, Mrs. Johnson, but I'll ask around. Maybe Deacon Gilbert knows." He said good-bye and hung up the phone, then turned around and told Argo about the call.

"That's strange," Argo commented. "Do you suppose it has anything to do with Jenny's dreams? I wonder what's going on."

"I'm sure it's nothing, but I promised Mrs. Johnson I'd inquire. I'll start by calling Deacon Gilbert." Mr. Jenkins turned toward the phone, picked up the receiver, and punched in some numbers.

"Hey, I heard you guys talking about me." Jenny ran into the room. Her new friend, Calvin, ran in behind her.

Argo told her about the phone call.

"I didn't think it was really a dream." Jenny turned to Calvin and told him about the piano music she had heard in the middle of the night. "Can other people have the same dream as you?" she asked Argo.

"I really don't know," Argo answered, "but I will have to admit that it is a strange coincidence."

"Can we have some cookies?" Jenny asked.

"Sure. Just be sure to close the tin tight," Argo answered. She smiled at the children.

Jenny and Calvin ran into the kitchen. Jenny's light brown ponytail trailed behind her like a long ribbon.

Mr. Jenkins hung up the phone and turned around. "No one has keys to the church except Reverend Stone, the secretary, and the custodian. Deacon Gilbert said that none of them play the organ. This gets stranger every minute."

"There's probably a very good explanation," Argo answered. "We just have to find it. In the meantime, I need to round up some girls. It's bath time." She got up from her chair and walked out into the kitchen.

Jenny had been asleep for some time when she woke up with a start. She heard piano music. She knew she wasn't dreaming. She pinched herself, just to make sure. "Ouch!" Jenny cried. Now she knew she was awake. She decided to check the piano to see who was playing it. Jenny crawled out of bed, slipped on her kitty slippers, grabbed her robe from the end of the bed, and tiptoed down the hall. She didn't want to wake anyone. She wasn't afraid, just curious. She started down the stairs and tried to keep her feet on the sides where the stairs didn't creak. The music got louder as she descended the stairs. She thought that it was Argo or her dad. They had both taken piano lessons when they were kids.

Jenny reached the bottom of the stairs. Her heart fluttered, not from fear, but from the excitement of what she would find. She peeked around the corner into the living room. Aunt Annie sat at the piano with a smile on her face.

"Aunt Annie!" Jenny squealed. She ran across the room with her arms outstretched. One of her kitty slippers fell off, but Jenny didn't notice. "I thought you were dead!" She put her arms around Aunt Annie, only to have them come right back and hug herself. She tried again, but her hands went right through her beloved great-aunt.

"I am, my dear," Aunt Annie smiled. "I just came back for a visit."

"I don't understand." Jenny scrunched her eyebrows together.

"I told God how much I missed my piano and my church organ. He told me that I should be happy in Heaven, that I deserved it. He let me come down last night to play here, then I went to play the church organ to satisfy my longing. I enjoyed it so much that God is going to let me come back to play my instruments until I find a piano that suits me."

"Aunt Annie, that's great." Jenny jumped up. "I'll go get Dad, so he can see you, too."

"No, dear." Aunt Annie pointed her finger toward Jenny. "You're the only one that's allowed to see me."

"Why?"

"I knew that you had musical talent, and I never taught you how to play the piano. I always wanted to, but I was going to wait until you were a little older. God has plans for you musically, and He wants me to teach you."

"Is that why I was the only one who heard you last night?"

"Yes, the only one here. Mrs. Johnson was allowed to hear me at the church, because she's the one who will find a replacement for Thelma Adams. God thought that if she could hear me play again, she might remember to find someone else who knows their way around an organ."

"I heard her play last Sunday," Jenny volunteered. "She isn't very good."

"I know, but she tries."

"That's what Dad said. When are you going to teach me?"

"We could start right now."

"Now? But it's the middle of the night." Jenny's brown eyes widened.

"That's the only time I can come."

"Okay, then, I'm ready." Jenny rubbed her hands together and smiled. "What do I do?"

For the next hour Aunt Annie gave Jenny lessons on the basics of piano playing. Jenny soaked up everything her great-aunt taught her, just like a sponge. It was as if she had played for months. She learned the scales, "Jingle Bells,"

"When the Saints Go Marching In," and three other fairly easy songs.

"I think that's enough for tonight, Jenny. You need to get some sleep before school tomorrow. I'll be back in a few nights. Meanwhile, practice everything I taught you."

"Okay, Aunt Annie." Jenny's bottom lip trembled. She felt like she was going to cry. "I wish you didn't have to go. I miss you"

"I'll be back, but remember, you'll be the only one who can see or hear me." Aunt Annie stood up and floated toward the front door, vanishing a little more with each step. She turned and blew a kiss to Jenny.

Jenny had tears in her eyes when Aunt Annie was no longer visible. "Good-bye, Aunt Annie. I'll do everything you say." Jenny knew that a miracle had taken place and wasn't sure just how to cope with her emotions. She was in awe of what had happened that night, and could only sit on the piano bench with tears of joy running down her cheeks, aware that she had been chosen to receive the miracle. She knew that she had to do everything in her power to learn to play the piano, for whatever reason she was chosen to receive the guidance. She sat without moving for a few minutes and thought about Aunt Annie. Jenny stood up, walked up the stairs, and crawled back into bed. She fell into a deep and restful sleep, waking only with Argo's gentle touch.

"Good morning, Jenny," Argo said. "Time to get up."

"Argo, I saw Aunt Annie last night."

"I'm sure it was just a dream, dear. Now, hurry. Breakfast will be ready as soon as I fix some toast."

"But I really saw her. She was downstairs playing the piano, and she taught me to play some songs."

"Sometimes dreams can be almost as real as life itself," Argo said.

"This wasn't a dream. It was real."

"We'll talk about this later. Now hurry, or you'll be late for school."

Jenny thought that she'd prove it to her by playing the songs she learned last night. She scrambled out of bed and dressed herself in blue jeans and her favorite red shirt. She skipped down the stairs as fast as her feet would go.

"Mercy, child. You're going to fall if you come down the stairs that fast," Argo called from the kitchen.

"I'm okay," she called. Jenny ran into the living room and sat down at the piano. She played all the songs Aunt Annie had taught her, without missing one note. She pounded on the keys so Argo would be able to hear her from the kitchen. When she had no reaction from anyone, she played the songs again, louder.

"When did you learn to play the piano?" Argo asked from the doorway, still holding the knife she used to butter the toast.

"I told you," Jenny smiled, "from Aunt Annie."

"Let's talk about this later when your father gets home. You need to eat and get to school."

"Okay, but someway I'll make you believe me." Jenny pouted behind Argo's back, stood up, and followed her to the kitchen. She thought that maybe her dad or Uncle Paul would believe her tonight.

CHAPTER FOUR

"CALVIN, WAIT UP," Jenny called. She ran down the porch steps and down the front sidewalk to catch up with her friend.

Calvin turned toward Jenny and smiled. "Hi. What's up?"

"I saw Aunt Annie last night," Jenny replied.

"How?" Calvin looked confused. "She's dead. I went to her funeral."

"I know. I was there, too."

Calvin squeezed his eyebrows together. "How could you see her last night?"

"I saw her ghost."

"Her ghost?" Calvin's eyes opened wide. "Cool!"

"You mean you believe me?" Jenny was surprised. Her own family didn't believe her.

"Sure. What's not to believe? My grandmother saw a girl ghost once. She sat in Grandma's rocking chair and brushed her hair with my grandmother's hairbrush. Grandma put her hands on her hips and told her to leave, so the ghost put the brush back on the dresser and faded away as she left the room. Grandma threw away the hairbrush after that. She couldn't stand the thought of using it again."

"That's how Aunt Annie left; just faded away."

"Ghosts are cool. I'd like to see one sometime."

"I'm glad you believe me," Jenny said. "I told Argo about it, but I could tell she didn't believe me, even after I played the piano."

Calvin turned toward Jenny with a surprised look. "I didn't know you played the piano."

"I didn't before last night. Aunt Annie taught me some songs when she came."

"Last night? We were in my treehouse last night until you had to go in and get ready for bed."

Jenny thrust her arms in front of her with her palms up. "I meant in the middle of the night."

"For real? My mom wouldn't let me get up and play anything in the middle of the night."

"No one knew," Jenny answered. "I heard piano music, and I got up and went downstairs to see who was playing. I'd heard it before, and I wanted to find out who was there."

"Well?" Calvin asked.

"Well what?"

Calvin squeezed his eyebrows together again. "Who was there?"

"Aunt Annie," Jenny replied. "She looked just the same as she always did, but I couldn't hug her. My arms went right through her." Jenny pretended to hug a ghost. Her arms went through the air and wrapped around her sides.

"Cool! Were you scared?"

"Not of Aunt Annie." Jenny looked up. She was surprised that they were halfway to school. She was so busy talking, she didn't realize they had walked three blocks.

Calvin pressed Jenny for more details. "Did she teach you the songs you played this morning?"

"Yeah. And she said she'd come back and teach me more."

"Cool!" Calvin turned toward Jenny and asked, "Can I come over and see her, too?"

"She said that I'm the only one that can see and hear her, except for Mrs. Johnson," Jenny explained.

"Who's that?"

"Mrs. Johnson lives next door to the church. She was able to hear Aunt Annie play a couple of nights ago."

"Did she see her, too?"

"No, she just heard her," Jenny answered.

"When's your aunt coming back?"

"I don't know. I guess in a couple of days. She told me to practice the songs until she comes back."

"This is so cool. I actually know someone who has seen a real live ghost."

"Ghosts aren't alive."

"Well, you know what I mean." Calvin sighed. "How are you going to convince your father and Argo about the ghost?"

"I don't know." Jenny turned and looked at Calvin. She put her finger on her lips. "Maybe I won't. I'll just let them wonder how I'm learning to play the piano. Later on they might believe me."

"Can I tell my mom?"

"Not yet. Wait until Dad and Argo believe me first."

"Okay. I promise." Calvin drew an imaginary X on his chest. "I won't say anything to anyone."

"You're a good friend, Calvin."

"Thanks. I'm glad you moved next door. There aren't any other kids on this side of the block, and Mom doesn't want me to cross the street to play with the Nelson kids. She said that they're wild and would be a bad influence on me. She doesn't want me to do the things they do."

Jenny turned toward Calvin. "Argo said the same thing. She's seen them ride their bikes after dark, cuss at the neighbors, and fight with each other. She said that I'll pick up bad habits from them."

By this time, Jenny and Calvin arrived at school. They ran into the playground to greet their friends. Neither mentioned the secret of Aunt Annie's ghost.

At the end of the school day, Calvin ran up to Jenny. "I've been thinking about what you told me all day. I couldn't concentrate on anything the teacher said."

"I know," Jenny replied. "I feel the same way."

Calvin looked confused. "There's one thing I don't understand."

"What?" Jenny spun around and faced Calvin.

"Well, how can your aunt play the piano if you put your arms right through her?"

"What do you mean?" Jenny answered with scrunched eyebrows.

"If she isn't there as a body with solid fingers, how can she play the piano? I mean, how can she push down on the keys?"

Jenny popped her forehead with the heel of her hand. "I never thought of that. I'll ask her."

"Can you ask her if I can see her, too?" Calvin asked brightly.

"You really want to see her, don't you?"

Calvin grinned. "Yeah. This is so cool."

"I'll ask her," Jenny answered. "It's possible. She told me lots of times that she thought you were a nice young man."

Calvin smiled. "I remember that she called me a young man. Are you going to go home and practice the piano, or can you play for awhile? I'm going to put a roof on my tree house this afternoon. I could use some help."

Jenny started to skip. Her long, brown ponytail bobbed up and down with each skip. "I'll ask Argo. I can practice after supper."

"If you can come over, bring a hammer. You can help me nail the plywood up for the roof."

"Uncle Paul has some old roofing shingles in the garage. I'll ask if we can have them." Her voice bobbed up and down with each skip.

Calvin had to run to keep up with his friend. "That's awesome. This is going to be just like a real house," he smiled.

"Maybe this summer we can camp out in it," Jenny suggested.

"Oh, I don't think Mom will go for that. She's so afraid that something's going to happen to me."

Jenny stopped skipping and turned toward Calvin. "What can happen in your own backyard?"

"Nothing that I know of, but Mom thinks someone is lurking behind every tree."

"I wish my mom was here," Jenny said. A tear ran down her cheek.

"Mom told me about the car crash that killed her," Calvin told her. "I don't know what I'd do without my mom or dad."

"Where's your dad? I haven't seen him at your house."

"Mom divorced him a couple of years ago," Calvin said with his head down. "She said that they didn't love each other any more, but I keep thinking it's something I did to make them split up."

"No, it is not your fault," Jenny said in a firm voice. She took hold of one of Calvin's hands and covered it with both of hers. "I heard my dad talking to Uncle Paul. He said something about your dad having a girlfriend, and your mom was mad about that."

"Maybe." Calvin met her steady gaze. "I've met his girlfriend. Dad is supposed to be living in a mobile home in Shady Pines, but when I went over to his trailer, his clothes weren't in the closet. They were over at Sandy's house, in her closet."

"Is Sandy his girlfriend?" Jenny asked.

"I guess she is. I never thought about who she was."

"Is she nice?" Jenny asked.

"She's alright, I guess. But I'd rather have Dad back living at home."

"I know what you mean. I love Argo. She's good to us 'n all, but, I really miss my mother."

"Argo's cool," Calvin answered. "She never treats us like kids. She talks to us like we're important, just as important as adults."

"Yeah, I know." Jenny smiled. "Let's run. I want to ask Uncle Paul about the shingles for the roof." Jenny took off in a sprint.

"Wait up!" Calvin called as he ran after her. His backpack flopped up and down on his back with each step.

"Catch me if you can!" Jenny yelled back, laughing. She ran faster. Her heart was beating with fierce thuds, but she was determined to win this race.

CHAPTER FIVE

AFTER JENNY ATE a dish of fruit salad and drank a glass of cold milk, she helped Calvin hold two pieces of plywood while he nailed them on the top of his tree house for a roof. They sat inside and admired their work until Argo called Jenny home for supper. She ate in a hurry and excused herself, then tried to carry an opened package of roofing shingles across her backyard. She dropped it halfway across. She let out her breath in a big whoosh. "Hey, Calvin. Com'on over and help me. This is heavy."

Calvin swung down from his tree house on a rope. "Look, I'm just like Tarzan." He jumped to the ground and beat his chest with his fists.

"Okay, Tarzan," Jenny laughed, "come and help me carry this."

Calvin ran to Jenny and picked up one end of the package. "This is heavy. How many are in here?"

"I don't know," Jenny answered. "Uncle Paul just told us to use what we needed and put the rest back."

"That's cool." Calvin looked confused. "I thought you were going to practice the piano after supper?"

"I am. I just came out to bring this over, in case you wanted to nail some up. I've got a bag of nails." She nodded toward the front pocket of her jeans. The package slipped from her hands and fell with a thud.

"I've got nails." Calvin dug into his pocket and brought out a long nail.

"These are shorter. Uncle Paul said that if we use long nails in the middle of the roof, we could get scraped on them when we stand up."

"I never thought of that," Calvin said. He rubbed his head as if he had scraped it on a nail.

"Uncle Paul said that the shingles need to be nailed from the edge of the roof first, with the dark color overlapping the light color when you put on the next one."

"Why?" asked Calvin.

"I don't know." Jenny twisted her mouth into a crooked shape. "I guess that's just the way shingles are put on." She picked up her side of the shingles.

"Okay. Thanks for bringing them." He picked up his side and walked to the tree house before he dropped it.

Jenny dropped her half of the load. "I'll help with the first couple of shingles, then I need to go home."

"Thanks," Calvin replied. He took one shingle out from the package and climbed up the wooden ladder he had nailed to the side of the tree.

"Hey, you forgot the nails." Jenny called. She grabbed another shingle and scrambled up after him. By the time she climbed halfway up, he was sitting on the plywood roof the two friends had nailed up that afternoon, holding his hammer.

"I guess we're pretty good builders," Calvin smiled. He pointed to the tree house roof with his hammer.

"Yeah," Jenny answered. "You'd better be happy we are. If we weren't, you'd be on the ground by now." She pretended to fall. Calvin pleased her with a laugh. Jenny smiled, handed him the shingle she had carried up the ladder, and dug in her pocket for the nails, holding on to the ladder with her other hand. "Uncle Paul said to let the first shingle hang just a little over the side, and then nail it down."

"Why?" questioned Calvin.

"I don't know." Jenny twisted her mouth and shrugged her shoulders. "That's just what he said."

"Okay. That's cool." Calvin nailed down the first shingle, then put Jenny's next to his, overlapping it the way Jenny had instructed.

"I'm going home now," Jenny said. She climbed down the ladder and jumped from the third step. She spun around and saluted Calvin. "I'll see you tomorrow morning. Argo wants to walk with us."

"Why?"

"She said she needs the exercise, but I think she wants to see how busy Custer Avenue is in the morning. I heard her talking to Dad about it."

"Okay," replied Calvin. "I'll see you tomorrow."

Jenny ran home and bounded up the back porch steps. She opened the door and burst in with one motion. "Hi, everybody!"

"I thought you were playing with your boyfriend," Marylou said in an uppity voice.

"Calvin's my friend, not my boyfriend," Jenny replied. "You're just jealous because there's no one your age around here."

"Jealous of Calvin? That's a laugh." Marylou turned and ran up the stairs.

Jenny was happy Marylou left. Now she could practice in peace. She walked over to the piano. She sat down on the bench then turned toward her father to ask him if it would bother him if she played, but he had fallen asleep in his chair. Jenny turned and played as softly as she could, running through all the songs Aunt Annie had taught her. After that, she played each one three more times, until she thought she knew them. She knew Aunt Annie would be happy about her progress. She wanted to please her.

Argo walked into the living room. "I thought I heard you in here, Jenny. I just made a blackberry cobbler. Do you want a bowl?"

"Sure." She smiled, jumped off the bench, and skipped toward the kitchen. "Do we have any ice cream?"

"In the freezer," Argo smiled, then called up the stairs to Marylou to see if she wanted to join Jenny.

Jenny slept all through that night. She didn't hear any piano music or anything else. She awoke disappointed the next morning. She wondered why Aunt Annie hadn't come. Jenny thought her beloved aunt had heard her play and didn't come because she needed more practice. She jumped out of bed and dressed quickly in blue jeans and her blue and white shirt. She ran down the stairs. Her heart raced when she jumped the last three steps.

"Mercy, child," Argo called. "You're going to trip and fall if you run on the stairs like that."

"I'm fine, Argo," Jenny laughed. "I always come down the steps like that. It's fun."

"I know, and I wish you wouldn't," Argo answered. "It worries me."

Jenny ran into the living room and sat down on the piano bench. She played all her songs again, twice, before Argo called her to breakfast. She hoped that Aunt Annie would come tonight. She'd be ready for her. She decided to practice some more after school, just to make sure. She was determined to play every song with perfection.

Jenny and Calvin didn't discuss Aunt Annie on the way to school. Argo walked with them and asked a lot of questions about the tree house, how safe it was, how strong the floor was, and if they were careful when they went up and down. Jenny assured Argo that they were careful and the tree house was strong. Calvin invited her over to see for herself.

After school, Jenny told Calvin that she was going home to practice. "I want my playing to be perfect when Aunt Annie comes back."

"That's cool," Calvin said. "I have to fix my bicycle chain when I get home. Can you come after supper and help me with the tree house?"

"I'm sorry. I can't. Argo's taking us shopping for new shoes." Jenny twirled around on her toes and kicked one foot into the air. She pointed her toes out as if she was showing off a new shoe.

Calvin laughed. "Okay. That's cool. I'll see you tomorrow." He turned toward his house and waved good-bye.

Jenny skipped up the walk to her house and hummed the first song she was going to play.

Chapter Six

Jenny awoke with a start to the sound of piano music. She knew that Aunt Annie was back and that she'd be surprised about her piano expertise. She knew all the songs perfectly. Jenny smiled and hopped out of bed. She was so excited that she didn't bother to grab her robe or put on her kitty slippers. She ran down the stairs and took the last three steps in a jump.

"My goodness, child, you'll fall taking the stairs so fast," Aunt Annie called from the living room.

Jenny laughed. "That's what Argo always tells me."

"You listen to her," Aunt Annie said. "She knows what she's talking about."

"I'll try," Jenny promised, "but it's fun running down."

"Come over here and sit." Aunt Annie patted the piano bench. "I want to hear your songs."

Jenny smiled and slid in beside her beloved great-aunt. "I practiced hard, and I think I know them." She put her hands on the keys and played the songs through, one after another without stopping, smiling and moving her body with the beat of the music.

"Jenny, I'm proud of you. You seem to be catching on fast."

"It's easy! I seem to feel the songs when I play them."

"I noticed that," Aunt Annie said. "Are you ready to learn some more?"

"Yes," Jenny answered. She rubbed her hands together. "I can't wait."

"I thought of the next series of songs you could learn, if you mastered the first ones. I don't think there's any doubt about that, now. There's some music inside the bench. Do you think you could get it out?"

"Sure." Jenny hopped up, and Aunt Annie hovered a foot or so above the bench. She opened the lid, poked her head into the bench, and asked, "What's the book called?"

"Marches for Young Children."

"Cool. I like marches." She found the book and closed the seat. She sat back on the bench and put the book up on the music rack. "What song should I turn to?"

"We'll start with the first two tonight." Aunt Annie turned and smiled at Jenny. "I wish we could have done this when I was alive, but there was no piano in your other house, and you wouldn't have had anyplace to practice."

"I like it this way. This is cool."

Aunt Annie smiled and put her hands just over the keyboard. She played the first march through, showing Jenny how it should sound.

"How do you do that?" Jenny asked.

"Do what, my dear?" Aunt Annie asked.

"Play without even touching the keys."

"I really don't know." Aunt Annie put her finger on the side of her eye. "I just think the notes, and the keys push down below my fingers. It's like my mind is telling the keys to play."

"Awesome."

"You try now, Jenny. These songs aren't much harder than you've already learned. The notes are about the same, but the mood is different."

"The mood?"

"Yes. The other songs had a different feeling than these. I saw how you moved with the music. These songs have a different beat, like one you could march to."

"You mean like 'Onward Christian Soldiers' that we march to in Children's Church?"

"Yes, exactly." Aunt Annie smiled and patted Jenny on her shoulder. "Jenny, you do catch on fast."

Jenny looked down at the hand, amazed that she could feel something, even though the hand seemed to sink right through her pajamas and shoulder. She felt that it must be one of those thought things Aunt Annie told her about. She thought she felt it, so she did. Weird.

"Is everything all right?" Aunt Annie asked. "You had such a strange look on your face."

Jenny smiled. "I'm fine. I was just wondering how I could feel your hand if it went right through me."

"Oh, dear. That is strange, isn't it?" Aunt Annie seemed to be lost in thought. "I'm new at this, too, so I can't tell you. I'm so used to patting my students on their shoulders when they do well, that I didn't even think about it."

"We can learn together," Jenny with a smile. She looked at the music and played the first line, with only one mistake. "Oops."

"That's okay. Try again." Aunt Annie patted her shoulder again.

Jenny played the first song through. She asked a few questions about the march beat, then, with Aunt Annie's help, she struggled through the second song. "That was hard, but I think I can do it," Jenny said. "I guess I'm tired."

"You should be," Aunt Annie replied. "We've been at this for almost an hour, and you have to get up for school tomorrow."

"That's okay." Jenny yawned and rubbed her eyes. "We don't have any tests tomorrow or anything."

"I'm proud of you, Jenny. You're doing so well."

"Thanks." Jenny stretched her arms above her head and smiled. "Did they find a piano that suits you yet?"

"I have one that's almost right. I need one that feels like this one."

"You're not going to take this piano back with you, are you?" Jenny looked alarmed.

"No, dear." Aunt Annie patted the piano. "This one stays here."

Jenny sighed with relief. "I'm glad. I'm starting to like playing it."

Aunt Annie smiled. "I'm glad, too, dear. I knew you'd be able to play."

"How did you know?" Jenny turned and stared at her beloved aunt with wide eyes.

"Just a feeling, I guess." Aunt Annie put her hand on Jenny's shoulder. "That's the biggest reason I'm allowed to come back. God knows of your special talent, too."

Jenny sat up straight. She felt proud. "I'll practice hard before you come back."

"I know you will." Aunt Annie reached over to hug Jenny. Her hands drifted right through her. "Oh, dear. There I go again."

Jenny threw her head back and laughed. "I guess this takes some getting used to, for both of us. When are you coming back?"

"I don't know. I'm playing for the Hallelujah Choir when I get back."

"The Hallelujah Choir?" Jenny was impressed. "Is that angels?"

"Yes, dear," Aunt Annie smiled. "I wish you could hear them. They have the most beautiful voices."

"Cool."

"Can Calvin see you when you come back?"

"Calvin, that nice young man next door?"

"Yeah. We're friends. He's the only one who believes me about you." Jenny looked sad. "I told Dad and Argo. But they think you were a dream that seemed real."

"I'll find out and tell you when I come back. God only gave permission for you to see me. Maybe Calvin could ask God."

"Ask God? You mean pray?"

"Sure."

"Cool." Jenny smiled, and her sadness seemed to disappear. "I'll practice hard before you come back."

"I know you will, dear. I'm so glad I've been given permission to come back. God only lets people come back who have unfinished business."

"Unfinished business? I thought I was finished." Jenny looked down at herself. She ran her hands down her sides to her legs.

Aunt Annie laughed. "You're a work in progress, dear."

"A work in progress?"

"That means that you're always learning something new, changing the way you do things, feel about things, and think."

"Oh."

"You go up to bed now. I'll be back." Aunt Annie stood up, hugged Jenny with her ethereal arms, and floated toward the door. She turned and waved before she faded away.

Jenny thought that she was part of a miracle. She stood up, smiled. and walked back up the stairs. She didn't feel the coolness of the air until she shivered as she pulled the covers up to her chin. She thought that she'd better practice hard, if God gave permission for Aunt Annie to teach her how to play the piano. She wondered why she was chosen. She thought of this, not coming to any conclusion, as she drifted off into a deep, sound sleep.

Chapter Seven

"Jenny, time to get up," Argo called from the foot of the stairs. "The pancakes are almost ready."

"Pancakes," Jenny said out loud. "I love pancakes." She jumped out of bed, pulled on some clean jeans and a yellow shirt, and ran down the stairs carrying her socks and sneakers. Her brown hair bounced up and down on her shoulders with each step. She jumped the last three steps and landed with a thud.

"Mercy, child. You're going to fall coming down the stairs like that," Argo called from the kitchen. She poured more pancake batter onto the griddle.

Jenny laughed as she ran into the kitchen. "That's just what Aunt Annie told me. Can you make a pancake in a cat shape?"

"Sure, but what do you mean about Aunt Annie?"

"I saw her last night. She taught me how to play some marches."

"I'm sure it was a dream that seemed very real to you, dear."

"No, I saw her, talked to her, and felt her hand touch my shoulder."

"Dreams can seem very real," Argo said.

"This wasn't a dream." Jenny stamped her foot. "I'll play you the new songs she taught me."

"Okay, but eat your breakfast first." Argo plopped three cat-shaped pancakes on her plate.

"These pancakes are cool, Argo. Thanks." Jenny tipped the bottle of blueberry syrup over her pancakes. The pancakes soaked up the syrup and turned purple.

"You're welcome." Argo smiled. "You'd better hurry, or you'll be late for school."

Jenny looked around the room. "Where's Marylou?" she asked between bites.

"Sharon called and wanted to show her some kittens. She left about ten minutes ago. They're going to walk to school after that."

Jenny jerked her head up. "Kittens! I love kittens. Can we have one?"

Argo smiled. "We'll have to talk to your father about that." She turned at the sound of pounding on the front porch steps.

"Jenny," Calvin called from the front door.

"Com'on in," Jenny hollered. "I'm almost ready." She stuffed the last bite into her mouth and picked up her socks.

"Do you want me to walk with you today?" Argo asked. "Do you think Pete still needs me?"

Pete was a lonely little boy who seemed to need a friend. Jenny, Calvin, and Argo had befriended him on the way to school one day. He was lost and didn't know which way to go. Argo had suggested that he walk with them. After that, Pete waited on that same corner every morning, so he could walk with Jenny and Calvin. Jenny was proud that Argo had been kind to Pete. She knew that he needed a friend. He looked so sad, and his clothes were only clean on Monday. He wore the same things all week. The other kids laughed at him and made fun of his clothes.

"You can come if you want to, but Pete doesn't cry as much any more. He still waits for Calvin and me most every morning."

"I guess I'll stay here today," Argo said. "Just let me know if I can help. I feel sorry for that boy." She put the griddle into some soapy dishwater, then cleared the dishes from the table. Argo looked toward Calvin. "I'm sorry, Calvin. I didn't ask you if you wanted some breakfast."

"That's okay," Calvin smiled. "I ate a bacon sandwich at home."

Jenny finished tying her shoes and grabbed her jacket from the hook and her backpack from the floor. "Bye, Argo." She opened the front screen door and skipped across the porch.

"Bye, kids," Argo called. "Be careful when you get to Custer Avenue. The cars tend to go too fast on that street."

"We will," Jenny called. She was happy that Argo cared enough to tell them to be careful.

Calvin slammed the door and ran down the porch steps after Jenny. They didn't slow down until they reached the sidewalk.

"I saw Aunt Annie last night," Jenny said as she skipped down the sidewalk. Her long hair bobbed up and down with each skip.

"Did you ask her if I could see her?" Calvin asked. He ran to catch up with Jenny.

"She said for you to ask God for permission."

"I could do that." Calvin smiled. "Did she teach you any new songs?"

"Yeah, some marches." Jenny slowed to a walk. She pretended to play an invisible piano. She pounded her arms down and marched to the beat.

"Marches are cool," Calvin said. He fell in step and marched beside Jenny.

"I told Argo, again." Jenny stopped playing her make-believe piano and put her hands on her hips. "She still doesn't believe me. She thinks I've been dreaming."

"She will," he answered with conviction in his voice. "When's your aunt coming back?"

"She didn't say." Jenny started running. Pete was sitting on the corner waiting for them.

Calvin ran after Jenny. "Are you going to tell Pete?" he asked.

"Not yet. He probably wouldn't believe me, either." Jenny slowed to a walk and stuck out her bottom lip and looked thoughtful. "I'll tell him when my family believes me."

After school, Jenny couldn't wait to get home to practice the piano. She left Calvin at the sidewalk and ran up to her porch. "I'll come over later," she turned her head and called. She ran up the steps and opened the front door. "Argo, I'm home!" Jenny yelled as she burst inside and tossed her backpack under the coat hooks.

"I'm upstairs, dear," Argo called. "There're some fresh cookies on the table."

Jenny ran into the kitchen. Oh, good, she thought. Chocolate chip. She picked up one and bit it in half. Then she poured a glass of milk. Grabbing two more cookies, she headed for the living room. She put the milk and cookies on top of the piano and opened the songbook of marches. She stuffed another cookie into her mouth, took a big gulp of milk, wiped her mouth with the back of her hand, and started to play. She made several mistakes the first time, even though she tried to be careful. The second time was better, and by the third time, she thought she sounded pretty good.

"Mercy," Argo exclaimed from the doorway. "You sure have picked that up fast without any lessons."

"But I have had lessons! Aunt Annie's been teaching me."

"That's what you've been telling me. But I don't understand it."

"Neither do I," Jenny replied, "but I'm glad she comes. It's so much fun to have her here. I miss her so much."

"Such strange happenings," Argo muttered. She turned and walked toward the kitchen.

Jenny played through her songs three more times, then she returned her glass to the kitchen. "I'm going to Calvin's. Is that okay?"

"Just come back when you see your dad grilling the hamburgers. What were you just playing?"

"Marches. Aunt Annie taught me two new songs last night."

"You really sounded good."

"Thanks," Jenny smiled. "See ya' later." She ran out the back door and down the steps. She didn't stop running until she was at the foot of Calvin's tree house. "Hi."

"Hi, yourself." Calvin poked his head out the door and motioned to Jenny with his hand. "Com'on up. I brought up two chairs and a plastic table from the deck."

"Cool." Jenny scrambled up the ladder. She poked her head through the doorway and looked from side to side. "The tree house looks cool with furniture. Maybe we can eat out here sometime."

"Did you practice?" Calvin asked.

"Yeah, and I think Argo's starting to believe me about Aunt Annie." Jenny ducked in the door.

"Is that good?"

"I guess so, unless she wants to come and see for herself. She won't see Aunt Annie. All she'll see is me, talking to the air."

"Why?" Calvin scrunched his eyebrows together.

"Aunt Annie said that I'm the only one who could see and hear her." Jenny plopped down on the chair across from Calvin.

"Oh. I almost forgot." Calvin thumped his forehead with the heel of his hand. "My mom wants to know if you could go to the movies with us tonight."

"What are you going to see?"

"Some space thing my mom read about."

"I'll ask Dad and Argo at supper. It should be okay since there's no school tomorrow." Jenny looked down. "Oh, no!" She put her hand over her mouth. "Here comes Marylou." She tried to hide. She scrambled off her chair and sat behind the wall by the doorway.

Marylou was running across the yard chanting, "Jenny and Calvin, sitting in a tree, K-I-S-S-I-N-G."

"We're not kissing." Jenny yelled down. "Leave us alone."

"Make me." Marylou put her hands on her hips and stood beneath the tree house. She stuck out her tongue just as Jenny peeked around the corner.

That made Jenny mad. She squeezed her fists together and squeezed her eyes shut. Then she picked up the Coke can that Calvin had put on the table, grateful that he hadn't finished it. She reached out the door and turned it over so the contents spilled on the top of Marylou's head.

"You little brat," Marylou yelled. "Why'd you do that?"

"I'm tired of you teasing me," Jenny cried. "Leave us alone."

"I'm telling." Marylou turned and ran home. She looked over her shoulder and saw Jenny standing in the doorway of the tree house.

Jenny turned to Calvin and said, "I guess that blows it for the movies tonight, but it was worth it."

Calvin laughed. "I wish I could have had a picture of her face when the Coke hit her head."

"That was pretty funny," Jenny smiled. "The bad thing about it is that I'll probably be grounded to my room tonight. Oh, well. I've got some new comic books to read and a book that I checked out in the school library."

"I'll climb up the Chokecherry tree by your screen porch and come over on the roof to your window after supper."

"What about the movies?"

"I'll ask Mom if we can go to the movies tomorrow, instead."

"Thanks. You're a good friend, Calvin. Wait till everyone goes in, so they won't see you." Jenny glanced over at her house. "I've got to go. Argo said to come home when my dad was grilling." She climbed partway down the ladder, then jumped the last three steps. "Bye." Jenny turned and waved at Calvin, then walked toward her house, with slow steps, knowing that she was in trouble. She was prepared to take her punishment. It wouldn't be too bad, she thought. Calvin will help her pass the time.

CHAPTER EIGHT

THREE DAYS PASSED. Jenny practiced the piano every day. She thought each night that Aunt Annie would return. She went to sleep with the expectation of hearing her aunt playing the old piano. Each morning she woke up and thought that she must have slept through the night without hearing her.

The third evening, Mr. Jenkins read in the living room while Jenny practiced her songs. She thought that she sounded wonderful when she pounded down, like someone was marching. She could feel the footsteps falling in her music.

Mr. Jenkins put his book down on his lap and asked, "Where did you learn to play like that?"

Jenny spun around on the piano bench and answered, "From Aunt Annie." Her dangling feet swung back and forth like she was on a swing.

"I know you've told me that, but I thought you'd been dreaming."

"Do people learn to play the piano in dreams?" Jenny asked.

"Not that I know of, but, I guess, subconsciously it's possible."

"Subconsciously?" Jenny squeezed her nose and squinted her eyes. "What does that mean?"

"It's a term to describe your thinking behavior or your mind."

"Oh." Jenny didn't understand what her father was talking about. She did know that Aunt Annie wasn't only in her mind. She knew Aunt Annie was real. "That's not how it happened," she said.

"Not how what happened?"

"Aunt Annie doesn't come to me in a dream. She came to our living room, played the piano, and talked to me. She taught me how to play the piano. First she played a song, then she helped me play it. Aunt Annie patted me on the shoulder when I did well."

"Wait a minute." Mr. Jenkins jumped up. His book tumbled to the floor. "She patted you on the shoulder?"

"Yes, why?" Jenny scrunched her eyebrows together. "Is that important?"

"She always patted her students on the shoulder. When I was a boy and took lessons from her, she would pat me on the shoulder."

"So?" Jenny asked.

"So, this is sounding more and more believable."

"Why?" Jenny scrunched her eyebrows together.

"For one thing, not many people can start playing an instrument like you've done without some type of instruction. Another thing is the patting on the shoulder. That's the way Aunt Annie taught."

"Teaches, Dad. She's teaching me now."

"I don't understand, but I'm starting to believe you."

Jenny smiled. "Thanks, Dad. Now two people believe me."

"Two?"

"Calvin always believed me."

"I'm sorry I didn't believe you at first," Mr. Jenkins said, "but this is an unusual happening."

Jenny stood up and walked over to her father and hugged him around his waist. "That's okay, Dad. I guess if someone told me that they saw a ghost, I probably would have a hard time believing them." She reached up and gave her father a quick kiss on his cheek, then ran toward the kitchen. She smelled something chocolate. She burst through the kitchen door just in time to see Argo taking a cake out of the oven. "Oo-oo! Cake. Can I have a piece?"

Argo put the cake on the table. "Wait until it's frosted, dear."

"May I go outside for a while?"

"Don't stay long," Argo said. "It'll be dark soon."

"I won't be gone long. I just want to tell Calvin something."

"Okay, if you come right back."

Jenny rushed out the back door, down the steps, and across the yard to Calvin's tree house. She was so happy to be believed that she had to tell someone, and she knew that Calvin would understand.

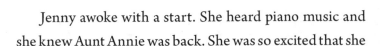

Jenny awoke with a start. She heard piano music and she knew Aunt Annie was back. She was so excited that she jumped out of bed and ran down the stairs, forgetting her robe and kitty slippers. She turned the corner and called, "Hi, Aunt Annie. I'm so glad you're back. I've practiced hard."

"I know you have, dear," Aunt Annie answered. "I've watched you."

"You watched me?" Jenny opened her mouth in surprise. "No way!"

"Yes, I did, several times."

"Do you know that Dad now believes me about you?"

"I'm glad, Jenny. He's stubborn, always has been. I knew that he would come around."

"You did? How?"

"Remember, I've known him a lot longer than you have."

Jenny looked serious. She pointed her finger toward her aunt. "There's something I've wanted to ask you."

Aunt Annie looked Jenny in the eye. "Yes, what is it?"

"Have you seen my mother?"

Aunt Annie nodded. "Yes, dear, several times."

"Could she come back with you sometime?" Jenny asked.

"She's been back," Aunt Annie said. "She had her time back on Earth like I have mine now."

"When was she back?" Jenny scrunched her eyebrows together. "I don't remember when she was here."

"You were very young, dear. Your mother told me that she came back when your Dad was trying to find someone to take care of you after she died. She helped find Argo."

"No way." Jenny shook her head.

"Yes, she did." Aunt Annie said. "Do you remember Mrs. Peterson?"

"No, but Marylou does. She told me how mean she was."

"She wasn't nice to anyone. Thank goodness your father told her to leave. I would have told her, if he didn't."

"I remember Evelyn. She had a weird boyfriend who used to peek in the window to spy on her. He scared me."

"I remember her. She was good to you, but she wasn't reliable."

"Why?"

"Well, for one thing, she wouldn't show up some mornings, and your dad would miss work."

"How did my mother help find Argo?"

"She knew about the trouble your dad had when he tried to find someone loving to take care of you. She looked and looked until she found Argo. Argo had been taking care of two children that had grown up and didn't need a nanny, so she was looking for another family that needed her."

"How did my mother tell Argo about us?" Jenny was excited to hear about her mother. She was killed in a car accident when Jenny was three, and Jenny didn't remember much about her.

"Your mother told me she worked through Argo's sister Mary."

"I like Mary," Jenny said. "How did she help?"

"Your mother made Mary see the ad in the newspaper about a nanny for you. She put a thought into her head that Argo would be perfect for that job."

"Awesome."

"It's getting late, dear," Aunt Annie said. "You won't be able to get up in the morning, and I'd like to hear you play your songs."

"Okay, but why can't my mother come back another time?"

"God only grants one time back for a person to finish something or to take care of a loved one."

"Oh, and she's had her time?" Jenny looked sad. She poked her bottom lip out. A single tear ran down her cheek.

"I'm afraid so, my dear." Aunt Annie put her hand on Jenny's cheek.

"I wish I could see her," Jenny said.

"You will, dear, when the time comes. Now, please play your songs for me before I go back tonight."

Jenny smiled, sat up straight, stretched her fingers, opened the music book and started to play. She played each march without an error. She played with a beat that sounded like people marching.

"That was lovely, Jenny," Aunt Annie said.

"Thanks." Jenny smiled. She was proud of herself. She knew she had to work hard if Aunt Annie had been granted permission to come all the way from Heaven to teach her how to play the piano. She wiggled on the piano seat with excitement.

"Would you like to work on more marches or tackle another type of song?"

"I like the marches."

"That's fine, let's go to the next song in the book." Aunt Annie played it through, then Jenny struggled through it. Aunt Annie played another, and Jenny followed. She tried to match the mood that Aunt Annie let flow through her playing. "That was excellent, Jenny," she said. Aunt Annie patted her on the shoulder.

Jenny smiled. "That's why Dad believes me now."

"Why's that?"

"I told him about how you patted me on the shoulder, and he said that's the way you taught." Jenny patted Aunt Annie's shoulder. "You patted your students on the shoulder when they did well."

Aunt Annie smiled at Jenny. "I'm afraid I didn't pat him much. He was always restless to go out and play."

Jenny laughed. "I'm going to practice so you'll be proud of me." She reached up and hugged Aunt Annie's neck, careful to stop in time, so she wouldn't go through her aunt's ethereal body.

"I know you will, dear. It's important that you work hard, for I don't know how many times I'll be able to come back." Aunt Annie hugged her. Jenny was amazed that she could feel her aunt's arms and feel her shoulder with her cheek.

"But I love when you come back." Jenny pulled back and looked at Aunt Annie with tears in the corners of her eyes.

"I love it, too," Aunt Annie said. "It's been important for me to be your first piano teacher. I know that you'll do well with the next one."

"The next one?" Jenny's eyes opened wide.

"Yes, my dear." Aunt Annie looked somber. "My time on Earth is limited. I'll only be back a few more times. In the meantime, I'll look for someone that will work with you, someone you will be able to relate to."

Jenny looked sad. A tear slid down her cheek and her lower lip trembled. "But I don't want anyone else. I want you to teach me."

Aunt Annie hugged Jenny. "I do too, but it has to be. Promise me that you'll work just as hard with someone else as you have with me."

"I promise, but I won't like it as much." Jenny managed a smile. She straightened up and wiped the tear from her cheek.

Aunt Annie laughed. "You are a very talented girl. I'm proud to be able to work with you, even if it's just a short time."

"Thanks." Jenny smiled. She felt proud that Aunt Annie said she was talented.

Aunt Annie pointed to the songbook. "Play the two new songs through once more, then you need to go back to bed."

Jenny played, smiling the whole time. She sat straight up and played the marches with only two mistakes.

"That was wonderful, Jenny." Aunt Annie smiled and patted her on the shoulder. "I have to go now, but I'll be back in a few days. Maybe I'll have some news about your next music teacher." She reached over and hugged Jenny, who tried to hug her back. Jenny was so excited that she found her arms meeting in the middle of her aunt's body. They both laughed. Aunt Annie stood up and floated toward the front door. "Tell your father to get the lock on the front door fixed. It looks just like it did when I lived here."

Jenny smiled and waved. "Okay. Bye." She tried to be brave, but she felt sad to see her aunt leave. Tears ran down Jenny's cheeks. She wiped them off with her fingers and said, "I'll miss you."

Aunt Annie faded out gradually, then disappeared altogether.

Jenny thought the visits were wonderful but strange. She found it a wonder that anyone believed her. It was hard for her to believe it herself. She turned off the light and walked up the stairs. She felt warm inside, happy to be part of a miracle, even if it couldn't go on forever.

Jenny whispered in a determined voice as she climbed into bed, "I'll show Aunt Annie, God, and everyone else what a wonderful piano player I can be. I'll practice and practice. Aunt Annie will not have wasted her time back on Earth. She'll be proud of me." She clenched her fist and held it up. Then she laid her head on her pillow and smiled. She fell asleep and dreamed happy dreams of concerts and playing the piano for the Hallelujah Choir.

CHAPTER NINE

"JENNY, WAKE UP," Argo called from the bottom of the stairs. "You're going to be late for school."

Jenny opened her eyes and scrubbed at them with balled up fists. She smiled when she thought of last night and Aunt Annie. The situation was still amazing, and she felt special that she had been singled out to receive such an astonishing gift. She jumped out of bed, dressed in jeans and a red t-shirt, and ran down the stairs, jumping the last three to the floor.

"Mercy, child," Argo called from the kitchen. "You need to be careful or you'll get hurt."

Jenny laughed. "I'll be okay. Don't worry, Argo." She skipped into the kitchen, her hair bouncing on her shoulders.

Mr. Jenkins looked over his coffee mug. "You sure are happy this morning, Jenny."

"I saw Aunt Annie last night."

"That's strange," he said with a faraway look on his face. "I dreamed about her."

"That's what Jenny's been doing, dreaming," Marylou said in a sassy voice. She poked a forkful of scrambled eggs into her mouth.

"Have not." Jenny spun around to face Marylou. She put her hands on her hips and leaned toward her sister. "Aunt Annie was here last night."

"Oh, sure." Marylou retorted. "You've seen a ghost, talked to a ghost, taken piano lessons from a ghost, and now I suppose you sent one into Dad's dreams."

"No, I didn't send her," Jenny said, "but she did say that she was trying to find someone else to teach me."

"Why?" Marylou asked. "Are you unteachable?"

"No. She said that her time here is limited, and she's trying to find me a permanent teacher. Maybe she entered Dad's dream to help him think about someone to teach me."

"Ha, what an excuse." Marylou started to get up from the table.

"Sit down, Marylou," Mr. Jenkins said gently. "I think that you ought to know that I believe Jenny about Aunt Annie."

"You believe her?" Marylou's eyes widened, and she stared at her father with an open mouth.

"Yes, strange as it seems, I do. She knows little things about the way Aunt Annie teaches piano that only her students could know."

"Like what?" Marylou asked.

"Well," Mr. Jenkins answered, "like the way she pats her students on the shoulder when they do well."

"That doesn't mean…"

"I know, Marylou," her father said, "but Jenny couldn't have learned to play the piano on her own, either."

"Well…" Marylou answered.

"I'm just saying that we need to keep an open mind about this," Mr. Jenkins said. "Maybe we should look at all angles. Maybe we need to listen to what Jenny's been telling us. We all know that Jenny doesn't lie."

"Thanks, Dad," Jenny said with a mouthful of toast.

"She does talk with her mouth full, though," Argo added.

Jenny gulped down the toast. "Sorry," she mumbled, then smiled. She turned toward her father. "Tell us about your dream."

"Aunt Annie wanted me to call Mrs. Rudy and ask her if she could take on you as an extra student after school."

"Mrs. Rudy?" Jenny asked. "Our school music teacher?"

"Yes," Mr. Jenkins replied.

"Cool." Jenny twisted her hair around her finger. "I didn't know that she taught piano lessons."

"I didn't either," Mr. Jenkins answered, "but I guess it won't hurt to call her. Did Aunt Annie say anything to you about getting someone else?"

"She told me that she was working on it because her time back here on Earth was limited. God granted her a special dispensation to come back to teach me, but that time is almost up."

"Did she tell you anything else?" Mr. Jenkins asked.

"She said that she's talked to Mom." A tear slid down Jenny's cheek.

"Can Mom come back, too?" Marylou butted in. "Can I see her?"

"I thought you didn't believe me," Jenny said.

"I guess I do." Marylou lowered her head. "If Dad believes you, it must be true."

Jenny smiled. "Thanks for believing in me, but Mom can't come back. She was granted one time back, and she's already taken it."

"When?" Marylou and Mr. Jenkins asked together.

"When you were having a hard time finding someone to take care of us after she died." Jenny looked at her dad. More tears welled up in her eyes.

Jenny and Marylou had two nannys before Argo came to live with them. Neither of them was the person Mr. Jenkins wanted to help him raise his little girls. They each only stayed a few weeks.

"I remember Mrs. Peterson," Marylou offered. "She was mean."

"I remember Evelyn," Jenny chimed in. "Her boyfriend peeked in the window at us." She put her hands over her mouth. "He scared me."

"How did your mother help?" Argo asked.

Jenny turned toward Argo and said, "She made your sister, Mary, see an ad in the newspaper that Dad had put in about a nanny. She put the thought in your sister's head that you'd be perfect for the job." Jenny smiled. "She was right."

"I remember," Argo said. She pointed at Jenny. "Mary came over to my house in that big car of hers waving the newspaper in my face as soon as I answered the door. She was so excited. I thought it was strange that she would even read the want ads, but when I looked at the ad, I thought it sounded perfect for me."

"It was perfect for all of us," Mr. Jenkins told her. He smiled and patted Argo's hand.

"Yes, it was," Marylou agreed. "I wondered how you found us. Now I know."

"It seems that your mother did some research before she found Argo, so that explains her time spent back on Earth." Mr. Jenkins looked sad. "I just wish that I could have seen her. I miss her so much."

"Me, too," Marylou echoed.

"Aunt Annie said that we will, when the time comes," Jenny answered.

"I guess we'll just have to wait," Mr. Jenkins added. "I'm just grateful that she found Argo. She's been good for all of us."

Argo had tears in her eyes. "Thanks, all of you. I appreciate that. I sure didn't know that Divine Intervention was the reason that I'm here."

"None of us did," Mr. Jenkins said, "but it all fits. You're perfect for us."

"Do you want to hear my new songs?" Jenny asked, changing the subject.

"Not now, if everyone is going to get where they are going on time this morning," Argo laughed. "I'll listen to you right after school."

"Jenny," Calvin called from the front yard. "Are you ready?"

"There's Calvin." Jenny jumped up and ran to the door. "I can't wait to tell him about everything." She opened the door and poked her head outside. "Com'on in, Calvin. I just have to put on my shoes and grab my backpack."

"Let me run a brush through your hair before you go out the door, Jenny," Argo called. "It won't take but a minute."

Within seconds the house was busy with people getting ready to go their different directions for the day. Each of them would keep the thoughts of the breakfast conversation with them, not just for the day, but for the rest of their lives.

CHAPTER TEN

FOR THE NEXT three days, Jenny went about her normal activities. She went to school, practiced the piano, played with Calvin, and went shopping for a new winter jacket; a red coat with white fur trim. She thought about Aunt Annie when she sat in Mrs. Rudy's music class. Mr. Jenkins had called Mrs. Rudy and asked about the possibility of Jenny taking piano lessons from her on Saturdays. She agreed.

Jenny told no one outside her family and Calvin about the nocturnal piano lessons. She was afraid that her friends at school would not believe her. After all, if someone told her about a ghost visiting them, much less giving that person music lessons, she didn't think she'd believe them. Calvin, on the other hand, did believe her, so they spent most of the time walking to and from school talking about Aunt Annie. On the days Pete joined them they would talk of other things.

On the way home the third day, Jenny and Calvin had just turned down their street and were within sight of their houses when Calvin announced that his mom had to go away for the weekend to help her mother move into an apartment. "Grandma can't do yard work anymore, so she sold her house and is moving into a retirement village."

"Are you going, too?" Jenny asked.

Calvin shook his head. "I don't want to."

"Why don't you stay with us?" Jenny offered. "Our sofa turns into a bed. You could sleep there."

"Would your dad and Argo care?"

"I don't think so, but we can ask." Jenny started skipping. Calvin had to run to keep up.

"I know my mom won't care," Calvin said. "I'd probably just be in the way at Grandma's."

"Let's ask Argo first," Jenny said, running up her front sidewalk. She opened the front door and burst into the living room calling, "Argo, I'm home." Calvin followed her inside and dropped his backpack.

"Hi, Jenny," Argo called from the kitchen. "I just took some bread out of the oven. Do you want some?"

"Sure. Yum." Jenny dropped her backpack next to Calvin's and skipped into the kitchen. "Calvin's here."

"There's plenty." Argo smiled. "He can have some, too."

"Thanks," Calvin said. "This whole house smells like a bakery. My mom never bakes bread." He sat down at the table with Jenny. Argo put butter and jam on the table.

"Jenny, would you pour some milk and get some plates?" Argo asked.

"Sure. Are you going to have some, too?"

"I think I will, but I'll have coffee with mine." Argo sliced thick slices of hot bread and put them on a plate in the middle of the table. She smiled as the children reached for the same slice of bread.

Jenny buttered her bread, letting the spread melt deep into the holes. She licked the warm butter off her fingers and asked, "Can Calvin spend the weekend over here? His mom has to go out of town."

"I know," Argo answered. "I talked to his mother this morning, and she told me about moving Calvin's grandmother. She said that she was going to take Calvin, but she was afraid that he'd be bored."

"Does that mean he can?" Jenny asked hopefully. She popped the last bite of bread in her mouth and licked her fingers.

"Well, we have to talk to your father and to Calvin's mom, but it's okay with me. Of course, he would do some errands with us tomorrow."

"I wouldn't mind that." Calvin smiled. He knew that every Saturday after errands, Argo took Jenny and Marylou to McDonald's.

"Let's go ask your Mom," Jenny said, jumping up from the table.

"Hold on a minute, young lady," Argo said. "We do have to clear this with your father first."

"Can you call him?" Jenny asked.

"No, but you could," Argo answered.

"Okay." Jenny jumped up, grabbed the kitchen phone, and punched in her father's work number. She talked for a few minutes and turned around smiling. "He said it's okay." She tugged at Calvin's sleeve. "Let's go ask your mom."

Calvin jumped up and followed Jenny out the door. Argo was still sitting at the kitchen table drinking her coffee when Marylou walked in.

"I just saw Jenny," Marylou announced. "She said that Calvin's spending the weekend here. Why?" Marylou asked.

"His mom's going out of town."

"That doesn't mean that he has to stay here. He's not bringing his snake, is he?"

"I hope not," Argo shuddered.

"It's bad enough that I have to put up with a little sister, now I'll have a little brother for the weekend, too."

"It won't be that bad," Argo told her. "Calvin's a nice boy. He won't bother you."

"Oh, yeah. Remember when Jenny poured Coke in my hair? She probably wouldn't have done that if she wasn't showing off for Calvin."

"It's only for two days," Argo said. "If you want to, you can have one of your girlfriends spend the night."

"Okay. Thanks." Marylou buttered some still warm bread and headed into the living room to use the phone.

That night, when Jenny was in bed, she wondered if Aunt Annie would come when Calvin was sleeping in the living room. She wondered if Calvin had prayed about seeing her aunt, and if permission was granted. Jenny hoped Calvin would be able to see her. After all, he was the only person who believed her at first. He never questioned the fact that she might be dreaming Aunt Annie's visits. It was good to have a true friend. Jenny smiled and wiggled deeper under her comforter. She said a short prayer, asking if Calvin could be granted permission to see Aunt Annie when he stayed overnight. Satisfied that she had done her best, she drifted into a deep and restful sleep. She dreamed of her mother in a long, billowy white dress with flowers in her hair. She awoke with tears in her eyes when she heard Argo's gentle call to breakfast. She missed her mother and wished she had never been in the car the day the drunk driver hit her. After she dressed, Jenny, for once, walked down the steps. Memories of her mother were filling her head, and she wanted them to last as long as possible.

Chapter Eleven

Calvin sat up with a start and rubbed his eyes with balled up fists. He heard music, piano music. He opened his eyes and looked right into the eyes of Jenny's Aunt Annie. He thought he was dreaming.

"Hello, Calvin," Aunt Annie said softly. "I didn't know you'd be here, but I'm glad you are."

"Are you for real?" Calvin asked.

Aunt Annie smiled. "Yes, dear, but just for tonight."

"Just tonight?"

"Yes, I'm afraid that this is my last time," she answered. "My business on Earth is finished. Now I can rest."

"Your last night?" Jenny yelled, coming into the room. "I don't want you to go!" She ran over to hug Aunt Annie with tears streaming down her cheeks. As usual, her arms went right through her beloved aunt. "Oops," she said, smiling through her tears, "I guess I'll never get used to that."

Aunt Annie and Calvin both laughed.

"It isn't my choice to come back or not to come back," Aunt Annie explained.

"I know," Jenny sobbed. "It's just that I'm going to miss you so much."

"I'm going to miss you, too, dear, but we'll be together some day."

"I don't think I can wait." Jenny rubbed the tears from her cheeks with the backs of her fingers.

"Sure you can, dear," Aunt Annie told her. "You have your whole life ahead of you. You can believe that God has special plans for your talent, if He allowed me to come back to get you started."

"I think she'll be known all over the world!" Calvin exclaimed smiling. "Will you still be my friend, Jenny, when that happens?"

Jenny turned toward Calvin and laughed. "I'll always be your friend, your best friend."

"Thanks." Calvin smiled.

"Do you want to play your last songs for me, Jenny?" Aunt Annie asked. "I'd like to hear them."

"Okay." Jenny walked to the piano and picked up her music. "I practiced every day. I wanted to make you proud of me."

"I know you did, and I've always been proud of you." Aunt Annie patted Jenny on the shoulder, only slightly going through the skin this time. "Oh, dear! I'm just getting the hang using of my ethereal body on Earth, just when I won't need it anymore."

Jenny and Calvin both laughed.

Jenny opened her music to the first march and played it through without a flaw. She made no mistakes until she was on the last song, then she hit one note of a chord wrong. Calvin couldn't tell that she'd made any mistakes at all, but both Jenny and Aunt Annie noticed it.

"That was wonderful, dear," Aunt Annie told her. "I'm so proud of you."

"Thanks," Jenny beamed, happy for the compliment.

"I've been saving a special song to teach you," Aunt Annie said. "It's one of my favorite hymns. Would you get the big red music book out of the bench, please?" She moved up a little and hovered just above the seat.

"Wow!" Calvin exclaimed. "How do you do that?"

"I really don't know," Aunt Annie smiled. "I guess it's one of God's little mysteries."

"Is it like when you play the piano and your fingers push the keys down without going through them?" Jenny asked.

"Yes, I guess it is." Aunt Annie answered. She put her fingers on her cheek. "I just think about playing the notes, and my fingers push down the correct keys, something like mental telepathy. I think about raising myself up and, lo and behold, I'm floating."

"Cool," Calvin said.

Jenny put the hymnbook on the music stand and opened it. "Which song did you want to teach me?" she asked.

"Turn to 'Rock of Ages.' I believe it's on page nine."

Jenny turned to the correct page. "This looks hard."

"It's really not," Aunt Annie answered. "If you'll notice, many of the chords are the same ones you've already learned. The only new part is the melody. I'll show you." Aunt Annie played the first few bars and explained each note as she played. "Now, you play what I played."

Jenny obliged. She played the short part with only one mistake.

"See, it's not so difficult, is it?" Aunt Annie patted Jenny on her shoulder.

"No, it's not," Jenny agreed. "It just looked hard at first."

Aunt Annie played a few more measures. She explained the song while she played. Jenny then played the part her aunt had explained. She played slower and made only one mistake.

"That's wonderful, Jenny," Aunt Annie patted her on the shoulder. She then played the rest of the hymn. "See if you can play the rest."

"Okay," Jenny answered, feeling more confident. She played the last part.

"Now, will you play the whole song through for me? I'd love to hear it before I leave."

"Okay." Jenny played the whole hymn, putting all her effort into her music. She wanted her aunt to be proud of her.

"That was splendid, Jenny. I'm so proud of you. By the way, did your father talk to Mrs. Rudy? I'm afraid I invaded his dreams the other night and put in a suggestion for him to call her."

Jenny laughed. "Yeah, he told me about that. He did call Mrs. Rudy, and she said that she could arrange her schedule so I could start next Saturday."

"That's wonderful, dear! She's very talented and a wonderful teacher. I did some research and visited several music teachers in the area before I decided on her."

"Did some research?"

"Yes, dear. I slipped in on several piano teachers while they were instructing their students, to see which one would be best for you."

"Cool." Calvin said. "Did they know you were there?"

"No, dear. The only people allowed to see me are you and Jenny. I just watched each teacher for a short time, and they didn't know I was there. I stayed invisible."

"Cool." He then asked with a worried look, "You mean at any time some ghost or angel could pop in and watch me without me knowing it."

"I guess it's possible," Aunt Annie answered.

"I think I'd better be good, or else I might be in big trouble." Calvin frowned, as if being good would be an enormous chore.

Jenny and her aunt laughed. Calvin joined in after a moment, having gotten the effect he'd wanted.

Aunt Annie turned toward Jenny. She took hold of both her hands. "I'm going to miss these little visits. I feel like I've been able to know you on a whole new level since I've come back."

"A new level?" Jenny asked.

"Just a different way, a special way."

"I know what you mean," Jenny said with tears streaming down her cheeks. "I'm really going to miss you."

"Work hard for Mrs. Rudy. Make me proud of your accomplishments."

"I will," Jenny promised. She rubbed the tears off her cheeks.

"I know you will, dear. Now come and give me a hug, one big enough to last a lifetime." Aunt Annie stretched her arms out. "You, too, Calvin. I'm so glad that you and Jenny have become such good friends."

Calvin jumped up and ran over to the piano bench. Aunt Annie put her arms around both children and smiled.

"I'm going to miss you, too," Calvin told her, trying hard not to put his arms all the way through her body.

"I feel good about leaving Jenny in such good hands. I couldn't have picked a better friend for her."

Calvin smiled. "Thanks."

"I'm afraid that I have to go now. I won't say good-bye, just so long for now. I'll see both of you again someday." Aunt Annie lifted her arms away from the children and floated up, just a little.

"Tell my mom I miss her," Jenny said.

"I will, dear." She leaned down and kissed Jenny on the forehead, then floated toward the door. She turned once and waved before she faded out.

"Awesome. Did she really come, or am I dreaming?" Calvin asked with wide eyes.

Jenny laughed. "She really came." A tear slid down her cheek. "I'm going to miss her."

"I know, but at least we can talk about it."

"Thanks, Calvin. Aunt Annie's right. I am lucky to have you for a friend. Com'on in the kitchen. Let's have some hot cocoa before we go back to bed."

"Okay." Calvin smiled. He loved hot cocoa.

The two friends walked into the kitchen. Jenny put some mugs with cocoa mix and milk into the microwave oven. The smell of cocoa was drifting out into the room when Argo walked in.

"I thought I heard you two. Why are you up?"

Jenny and Calvin both tried to tell her what happened.

"Whoa. Slow up. One at a time." Argo put a mug of cocoa for herself into the microwave and sat down at the table with Jenny and Calvin. They told Argo all about the events of the past hour in detail. They were both excited about telling their story, both happy to be believed. All three of them understood that a miracle had taken place over the past several weeks and knew that they would remember it forever.

Jenny, for the first time in her life, realized that death is not the end of life, only a new beginning. She missed her mother and Aunt Annie, but she knew they were just in another dimension, and she would see them again one day. She knew why Aunt Annie died with a smile on her face; she had a glimpse of her new beginning and those that were waiting to greet her. Jenny was determined to keep her memories of her mother and Aunt Annie alive and wanted to make both of them proud of her. She would use the piano to do this, for if God thought enough of her talent to let Aunt Annie use her time back to teach her, she wasn't going to waste such a miracle.

Epilogue

Jenny and Calvin remembered Aunt Annie's visits for many, many years. They talked of the miracle many times during their growing up years. Jenny and Calvin shared many adventures and remained fast friends, even after their college years.

Jenny became a concert pianist who specialized in gospel songs. She produced many CDs and used her story of Aunt Annie's visits to encourage young pianists as well as people who were afraid to die. She spent many years encouraging people in hospitals and nursing homes to realize that death is not an end.

Calvin became an architect who designed tall buildings. He also shared the story of Aunt Annie and was responsible for changing the attitudes of death for many people.

ABOUT THE AUTHOR

Ann Westmoreland

Ann Westmoreland lives near a small town west of Atlanta, Georgia. She grew up in northern Illinois, graduated from Rockford College with a master's degree in elementary education, and taught elementary school in Illinois, then moved to Georgia and taught until she retired. She is married with four children and six grandchildren and one great grandson.